Rapunzel

tiger tales

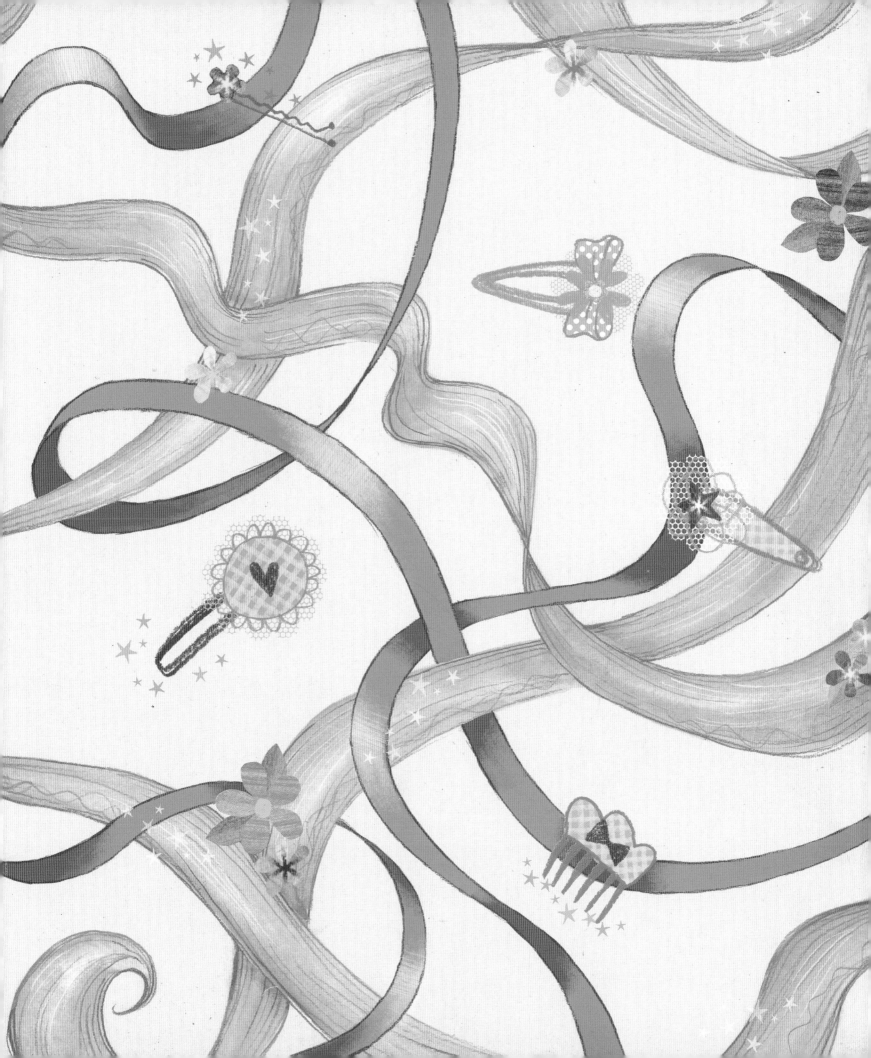

For Ada ~ my beautiful baby with rosy-gold hair ~ S. S.

For Elodie with love ~ L. S.

tiger tales
5 River Road, Suite 128, Wilton, CT 06897
Published in the United States 2019
Originally published in Great Britain 2019
by Little Tiger Press Ltd.
Text adapted by Stephanie Stansbie
Text copyright © 2019 Stephanie Stansbie
Illustrations copyright © 2019 Loretta Schauer
ISBN-13: 978-1-68010-119-5
ISBN-10: 1-68010-119-6
Printed in China
LTP/1400/2386/1018

For more insight and activities, visit us at
www.tigertalesbooks.com

FAIRY TALE CLASSICS

Rapunzel

adapted by
Stephanie Stansbie
Illustrated by
Loretta Schauer

KEEP OUT!

tiger tales

Bessie and Bert Greensmith loved each other very much.
But something was missing. And that something was a child.
"Why so glum, precious one?" Bert asked one day.
"I've been thinking," Bessie said. "I really wish we had a baby."

Bert thought for a while. "The neighbor's garden
is packed with delicious vegetables. You know what they say:
Eat your greens — they'll make you great.
So pile some veggies on every plate!"

"Please don't go next door," Bessie said to
Bert. "That lady seems like a bit of a witch."

But Bert wanted a child as much as his wife. So one moonlit night, he . . .

picked a pepper . . .

lopped a lettuce . . .

and bagged some beets!

And guess what? The following year, Bessie and Bert had a **bouncing** baby girl.

But that night, something terrible happened.
The witch from next door snuck into the house
and took the baby away.

"Steal from me, and I'll steal from you!"
she cackled (as witches do).

Then she built a dingy, doorless tower deep in the darkest woods and hid Rapunzel inside.

Rapunzel was lonely, of course. But she also grew up to be very inventive.

She had to be, locked in a tower all day!

La La La La LA

La

La La

She built herself a model
railroad, a unicycle, even
a telescope, and made up
hundreds of songs.

When the witch came to the tower,
she stood at the bottom and yelled:
"Rapunzel, Rapunzel, let down your hair!"
Rapunzel's rosy-gold hair had grown so
long that all the witch had to do was
climb up. It was very uncomfortable.
But Rapunzel was used to it.

"When can I go out and explore?" she asked every single day.

But the witch always had the same answer: "The world is full of rascals and robbers. They'll steal the hair off your head."

One day, a prince was hunting in the woods
when he heard Rapunzel's voice.

La La
La
La

What an incredible singer, he thought,
gazing up at the tower. *But how do
I get up there?*

Just then, he heard someone shuffling along the path toward the tower, so he dove into the bushes. When the witch reached the tower, she called, "Rapunzel, Rapunzel, let down your hair!" And as she scaled Rapunzel's lustrous locks, the prince was flabbergasted. *Now I've seen everything!* he thought.

BUGS

Once the witch had left,
the prince called up:
"Rapunzel, Rapunzel,
let down your hair!"

"Who are you?" Rapunzel yelped when she saw the prince at her window.

"I'm Freddie," said Prince Freddie. "Can I come in?"

"Depends if you're going to steal something," Rapunzel said. "I'm a black belt in karate, you know— self-taught!"

But Rapunzel decided to show him all the things she'd made.

They talked and talked. Prince Freddie
was funny, and he knew SO much stuff.

But then the witch came back.

Prince Freddie held out his hand to her.
"I'd like to take Rapunzel to the palace," he said.

The witch's face was dangerous and dark.
"Steal from me, and I'll steal from you," she hissed.

Then
she
hurled
him
out
of
the
tower!

"You'll never leave this place," the witch snarled. "You're mine." And she jumped out of the window, yanking hard at Rapunzel's locks.

Nobody owns me,
thought Rapunzel.
Then she cut off her
rosy-gold hair, tied it
to the window, and
sailed down.

When Rapunzel found Prince Freddie, he was battered and blind. "I'm so sorry," she sniffed, wiping her eyes.

"It's not your fault," the prince smiled. "Please don't cry."

But Rapunzel's tears
were like magic.

Prince Freddie blinked.
He could see again!

Cool haircut!

Back at the palace, Prince Freddie made Rapunzel
his **Chief Inventor**, and they became best friends.

Rapunzel built all kinds of cool things for the kingdom—
even a harvesting machine. Then she offered
free vegetables to everyone in the land.

And guess what?

She gave the witch
the job of giving
away the veggies!

WELCOME

FREE

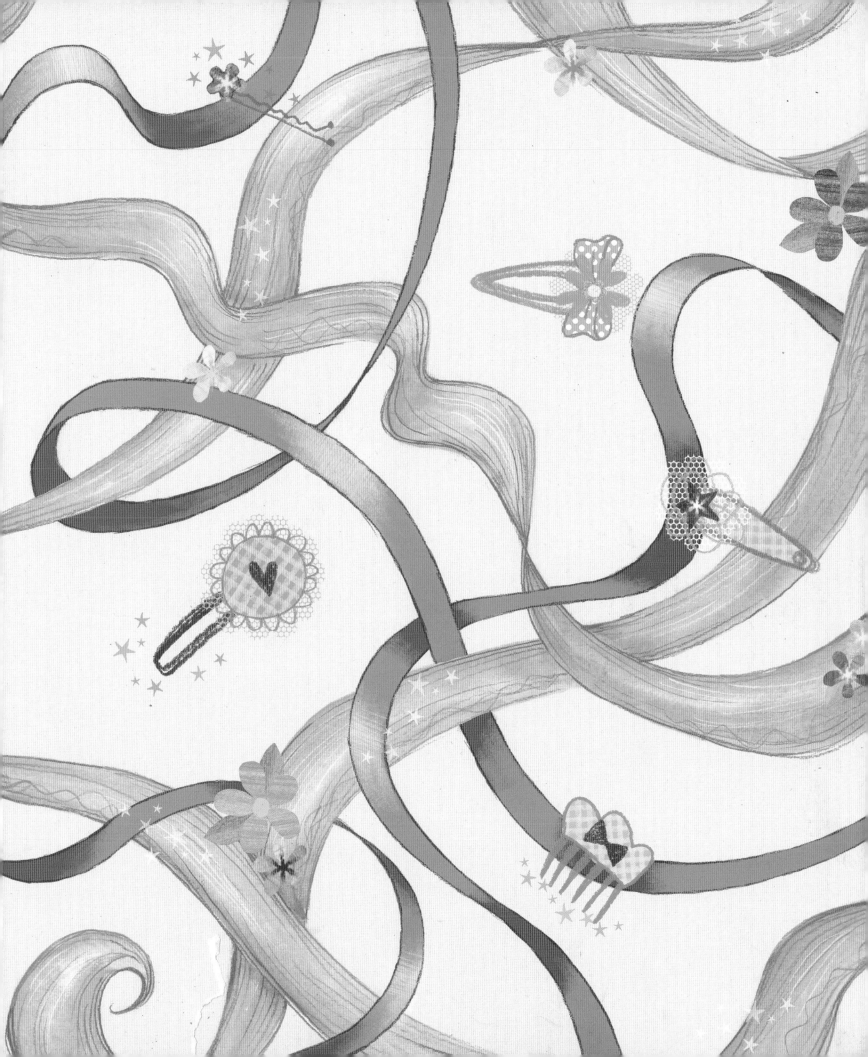

Stephanie Stansbie

Stephanie has never stopped loving fairy tales.
She has written a number of picture books, as well as a nonfiction
book called *Dinosaur*. In her spare time, she enjoys capoeira
and spending time with her family.

Loretta Schauer

Loretta began her journey into children's illustration
through attending evening classes. She has always loved drawing
and is never happier than when she's making something.
Loretta lives in London, England, with her husband and her
irrepressibly confident hamster studio buddy, Nanook,
who assists with the creative process by staring really hard
at her until she gives him a treat.